Frontiers and Pioneers

Canadians in a Far Country

by Terry Leeder

illustrated by
Deborah Drew-Brook

design by
Ron and Ron design consultants

Toronto
Dundurn Press
1979

To Ken

Dundurn Press wishes to acknowledge the generous assistance of the Canada Council and the Ontario Arts Council.

Dundurn Press Limited
P.O. Box 245, Station F
Toronto, Canada
M4Y 2L5

Canadian Cataloguing in Publication Data

Leeder, Terry, 1937-
  Canadians in a far country

(Frontiers and pioneers)

ISBN 0-919670-44-X pa.

1. South African War, 1899-1902   - Canadian
participation - Juvenile fiction. I. Drew-Brook,
Deborah. II. Title. III. Series.

PS8573.E3455C35   jC813'.5'4   C79-094676-9
PZ7.L44Can.

THE DOCTOR

Chapter 1
Rooinek

Beyond the rectangle of the doorway, the sun seemed to soak down on the dust. Fred Livingston handed the two boxes he had finished packing to his servants. The Zulus carried them outside, and set them down on the ground, waiting for him to come out.

Five years earlier Livingston had come from Canada to South Africa. He was a medical doctor, and he worked in Zululand, among about 25,000 natives. But now in 1899 war had begun.

Livingston looked around the house. It was a shame to leave, he thought, but he had no choice. He walked to the door, squinting in the bright sun, put a soft, broad brimmed hat on his head, and stepped out. The servants watched him, but noticing that he stood there looking towards the mountains, made no move to pick up the boxes.

To the north, hazed with distance and looking like greyish-blue mounds, were the Lebombo Mountains. Beyond them was the Boer Republic of Transvaal.

The Boers were tough farmers, Fred Livingston knew. They could ride, shoot, knew the country and spoke a special brand of Dutch they called Africaans. They were at war with the British, and since Livingston was working in the British section of South Africa, hundreds of Boer commandos were headed in his direction.

Somewhere on the ocean, a corps of the British army was steaming towards South Africa. But there were hardly any British troops on the spot. That's why Livingston had to clear out. Well, he thought, this is going to be a war between white men, even though there were thousands more black Africans than whites in South Africa.

It's a long way from Canada, Livingston thought, as he walked over to his horse, which one of his servants had saddled and led out to the shade of a tree. It was a strong, lively horse, but Livingston liked an animal with lots of spirit. He had draped a couple of blankets over his shoulders, and now threw them over his horse's neck. He'd be sleeping in the open and so he'd need the blankets. Just an hour earlier, a Zulu runner had come in and announced: "The Boers have crossed the mountains."

"How many?" Livingston had asked.

"Three hundred."

The magistrate, the clerk, and the police officer who worked on the Zulu reserve had fled to the bush. Livingston had taken his time. After all, he reasoned, I'm a doctor, not a fighting man.

As he swung into his saddle, Fred Livingston still felt no need to hurry. He knew a lot of these Boers, for he had treated their illnesses. So what did he have to worry about?

He flicked the reins, and his horse started off. He decided to head for the nearest British police post. Behind him, the low buildings of the court house receded. His horse tossed its head, to let Livingston know it wanted the load off its back. It was used to taking the doctor on rides around the country, but not the extra weight it carried now. The doctor kept a close grip on the reins, and forced the animal to head west. About two and a half kilometres from the court house, he stopped, dismounted, and took the blankets off the horse's neck. His two servants had followed on foot, carrying the boxes, and he decided he'd also give them the blankets to carry.

The ground right here was uneven, with boulders and scrub brush jumbled on both sides of the path that snaked west. Livingston draped the blankets over a bush, then lifted one of them by the middle, and started to fold it up to make a smaller bundle for the servants to carry.

The clatter of some stones, and the noise of brush being pushed aside made Livingston look up. A large number of riders had just come around the nearest bend in the path, and he stared into the barrels of several rifles.

The riders wore scruffy clothes of all colours and cut. Most of the men had scraggly beards, and all were tanned and wrinkled from farming on the African veldt. They had wide brimmed hats, and belts of ammunition slung crossways over their chests.

"Rooinek," said one of them. That was Dutch, thought Livingston, and it meant 'red-neck', which was the term that Boers used to describe Englishmen.

He couldn't run, Livingston thought. By now, more riders had come up and levelled their guns at him. It would be insane to try to fight, and his horse was tied up to the branch of a small tree. They'd caught him dismounted. But why, he thought, had they come from the west? He wasn't expecting them that way at all.

Fred Livingston walked very carefully towards them, making sure he held his hands in sight. They lowered their rifles, and one of them dismounted, came up, and shook his hand.

"Well, Doctor, you may thank your stars I'm

here. Otherwise, you'd be dead by now."

He was a man Livingston knew well. He'd come to Zululand six months before as a labour agent, in order to hire men for work in the mines of the Transvaal. Only a week or so before, this same man had eaten breakfast in Livingston's home. And all the while, thought Livingston, he was spying.

So, for the rest of that day, the medical doctor from Canada sat on the ground in South Africa, guarded by four Boer farmers who had turned soldier. Black smoke boiled up from the court house and the house Livingston had left that morning. He looked at the ravines and the lush green hills beyond, and could hardly believe he was in the middle of a war. Once in a while, some Boers would come up, dismount, and ask him about a herd of cattle that had been nearby until a few days ago. He shrugged, and they said things in Dutch that were not complimentary.

The afternoon darkened into evening, and then the night came on. The Boers changed his guard, and the glowing embers from the smoking ruins of his own house lightened a patch of sky to the east. There were no stars. From the sea which was some kilometres to the south, a dense fog seeped in. The hills vanished in white, then the ravines, then the trees, until only the figures of the guard were visible, their rifles across their knees. They watched Fred Livingston with distrust. And he began to feel very uneasy.

Chapter 2
Prize Chickens

"You might have got clear away," said the man that Fred Livingston knew. He sat down beside the prisoner. "I suppose you thought we would come in direct from the north. Most of us did. But some of us peeled off west to cut the telegraph wires, and we came in by the same path you were taking out, it seems. Bad luck."

The man got up and went off to a group who had ridden up with live chickens tied across their saddles. They killed the birds, and the farmers sat and started pulling off the feathers for an evening meal.

Those were the prize chickens that had been kept by the magistrate, Livingston thought. He wondered what the magistrate's feelings would be if he were here.

The men cracked dry sticks and brush, and piled them loosely under some pots taken from the houses. A match snapped, and flame swayed among the sticks. After a little time, steam curled from the pots, and the water popped and danced. A chicken was plopped in each pot.

The magistrate's prize chickens smelled good, thought Livingston. He remembered his stomach, and it told him he hadn't eaten since early morning. Light glowed on the face of an old bearded farmer, and Livingston hoped that the old man would share some of their food.

He didn't.

Livingston began to worry about what was going to happen to him. In the morning, they'd start off for the Transvaal. He'd likely wind up in Pretoria, where they'd throw him in jail, where he'd stay for month after month. Perhaps he would die of sickness — or lack of food before the British army finally showed up and surrounded the city. Or maybe he would be killed by a British shell when their guns opened up on the Boers. Or maybe he wouldn't make it that far — maybe some fellow would take it into his head to shoot Livingston on the way there. War let loose some terrible emotions. The Boers were angry at the British right now — at anybody British, or anybody speaking English, for that matter. He would be the only one handy.

While he sat there thinking of all this, he could smell delicious chicken. Nobody offered him any. The land was as dark as his mood. There were no stars, a dense fog, and seventy-five fully armed Boers all around him.

What were his chances of escape? It was intensely dark. He had ridden or walked over all of this ground for the past eighteen months, and he knew every stone and shrub and tree all around. Just a short distance away were a number of large rocks, and there was a spring of water bubbling up among them. Beyond that were a bunch of shrubs and a number of large trees. The ground broke sharply at that point, and sloped down to a ravine. If he could make a run for it, and get into the cover of those rocks and the ravine—

He tried to call up an exact mental picture of the landscape around him in the dark. He could see the way the rocks were placed, the marks on their surface, the stream, the trees, and the place where the ground sloped. How many paces would it be, over to the rocks, for a man running for his life? If he tried and didn't make it, they'd shoot him for certain.

Yet — he spoke Zulu well and knew the ways of the people. He was sure the Zulus would hide him once he got free. His health was good. He could rough it. And he knew the country pretty well from here to the nearest British police station. If he got away, he'd head for Pietermaritzburg.

He looked around him. The fog had lifted a bit, and he could see the Boers scattered around. None of them were farther away than a hundred metres, and some were quite close by. Some were already lying down asleep, others were grooming and feeding their horses, others were eating. If he reached out, he could touch the men who were guarding him. Their loaded rifles were resting on their knees. They hardly said anything to each other, and nothing to him. They seemed pretty grim.

But now he couldn't get the idea of escape out of his head. He would try it.

One of his servants walked between two of the fires carrying a bucket of water, and set it beside a Boer, who raised the bucket to his mouth. I can't leave my servants without warning them, Livingston thought. One of them lived in a Zulu village close by. He could get away all right. The other one was a Christian who had served Livingston for four years, and had stuck by even after the Boers captured the doctor. He was the one carrying the bucket.

A little while later, he passed close by with the water, and Livingston told the guards: "I'd like some water, if I could."

One of them shouted to the servant, who came over to Livingston with the bucket.

"I don't have anything to drink with," said Livingston, talking in Zulu. "Could you lift it up so I can drink?"

The servant did, and the doctor took the bottom lip of the bucket in both hands. Glancing at the guards to make sure they weren't looking, he held the bucket so the water wouldn't spill out. "I'm escaping," he whispered.

The servant looked him in the eyes, but said nothing. His expression didn't change, but Livingston knew he had heard. He lowered the bucket, and said out loud, "Thank you."

The Zulu nodded, turned, and carried the bucket away.

Livingston stretched out, pretending that he was settling down to sleep. He waited.

The fires gradually dimmed. Most of the men had laid down, and many were already asleep. There was dense night all around. One of the guards placed his rifle on the ground and stirred the fire nearby. Two more were sitting with their rifles on their knees, and the fourth one had rested the butt of his weapon on the ground, and held the barrel in his hand.

Fred Livingston thought about exactly what each man would have to do to raise his gun to his shoulder and fire a shot. He could see each action, how the muscles in their arms would react, how the rifles would be raised, the hands shifted into position, the butt snugged against the shoulder, and the finger squeezed on the trigger. One or two, or maybe ten seconds would pass before they realized what was happening. And then three seconds to raise the rifle, stand, and turn in the direction he was running.

Fifteen seconds — he might have that long.

Fred Livingston sprang to his feet. His legs were pumping, the darkness was suddenly around him, the ground flying beneath him, and Dutch voices howling behind him. He leaped, and flung himself prone on the ground behind the rocks. He lay there for a few seconds. Nobody fired. His sudden escape had stunned them. He jumped up again, leaped the stream, clattered down the ravine, across, up, through the trees, and around rocks.

His foot hit a stone, he fell, and his leg struck a sharp rock, but he jumped up, ran full tilt into a tree, dashed around it, and ran on.

He didn't care, he didn't feel any pain, for the dark was around him and the Boers behind him.

He had escaped.

Chapter 3
Swart Kop

A cluster of soldiers in khaki, with puttees wrapped on their legs, and domed pith helmets wrapped in khaki cloth on their heads, stood in front of the government office at Pietermaritzburg. Livingston had seen a train full of troops pass through the railroad station on his way in, so he guessed there must be fighting to the north. An officer was seated at a table in one of the rooms inside the government office. He bent over a list, and a small line of men stood in front of the table as he took their names down. Livingston joined the line.

"I'm a doctor," he said when his turn came. "I'd like to offer my services at the front."

"That's good of you, doctor," the officer replied, "but we've had a number of medical men from Johannesburg They cleared out when the Boers started fighting, and they've already signed up."

Since the officer seemed busy with his lists, Livingston nodded and went out again.

"Signed up, sir?" one of the soldiers outside asked.

"No. It seems they have enough doctors," he answered.

"I'm sure we'll need you later, sir."

"The officer didn't seem to think so," Fred Livingston went on. "What's happening?"

"Up front sir? No one knows. The Boers have still got the army surrounded at Ladysmith and pretty well every place else. Maybe the generals back in London don't take the Boers too serious. But we do sir. Still, we'll get 'em out when the boys from home arrive."

"Where are you from, sir?" one of the others asked.

"Canada."

"Fine show, sir," the second one replied. "They've just sent out some men to give us a hand."

"Them, and Australia, and New Zealand," the first put in. "There won't be much to do by the time they get here. We'll see to that, sir."

Livingston chatted a bit more, then tipped his hat and strode away down the street towards the train station. The street was wide and dusty, and the sun made a black shadow in front of him. Beyond the outskirts of the town, the hill they called Swart Kop stood up like a great wave at sea, and the clear blue South African sky stretched away behind it.

Livingston decided he might as well go back to Canada. Dear old Canada, he thought, suddenly very homesick. There wasn't much doing for him here. They didn't need him, so why stay.

It was a job now for soldiers.

THE SOLDIER

Chapter 4
Private Jack Randell

In the harbour of North Sydney, Nova Scotia, the square-rigged sailing ship, *Arcot*, was tied up. Jack Randell, the second mate, was sitting in the captain's cabin playing cards. The captain's wife and her sister had joined them. It was a cold, dark November night.

"Why don't you go to South Africa?" the sister suddenly asked, looking at the captain and Jack in turn.

The captain was a giant of a man, six feet eight inches tall, and he weighed three hundred pounds — all of it muscle. He slapped a card down, and said something in a voice blurred with anger.

His wife wasn't shocked at what he'd obviously said — after all, he was a sailor. But she didn't like it either.

Jack Randell, though, started to think about what the sister had said. He was a little past twenty, he had sailed to South America, England, and Labrador. His father was Captain Isaac Randell, a popular and well-respected man in Trinity, Newfoundland. Jack himself was always one for adventure.

The next morning, he knocked on the door of the captain's cabin, and stepped in when the captain answered. "I want to join up for South Africa, sir."

The captain swore. "I'll put you in hospital for a month if I catch you trying to join up," he barked.

"There are plenty of fools getting killed without you going too." Jack looked the big burly man over and didn't argue. The captain could put a man in the hospital all right! So he listened to the orders the captain gave, said, "Aye sir," and left. He waited until the captain went down for breakfast.

Immediately, he climbed to the deck. slipped ashore, and dashed for the ferry connecting North Sydney with Sydney. He went straight to the armory.

"How old are you?" the officer asked.

"Twenty-one," said Jack, telling the lie with a straight face. He was pretty sure he'd get on. You had to be tough to be a sailor, and he could use a gun and ride a horse too.

They took him down to the army stores and handed him a blue uniform, with red stripes down the legs, and a little yellow and blue pill-box hat. When he was all fitted out, he went to the telegraph office and wired his parents in Newfoundland, to tell them he'd enlisted. He returned later, got the reply, folded up the message, and slid it in the breast pocket of his tunic.

Holding himself erect and proud, Private Jack Randell marched to the ferry and crossed to North Sydney.

The captain glared at him as he climbed over the side and came up to his old skipper. "I've joined up, sir," Randell said, knowing he didn't have to tell anybody. The uniform said it all. "I'd like to draw my pay."

"Not a cent," shouted the captain as his face turned red with rage. Jack was astounded. What was this all about? But then he got angry himself, stamped off the ship, and went to the American vice-consul in Sydney.

The *Arcot* was an American ship, and Jack knew he could make trouble if he didn't get his pay. The vice-consul listened, smiled and said, "You'd better tell the captain he'd be wise to pay you off without making trouble. You can't make a crime out of a man enlisting."

Randell went back to the ship, and the captain slapped his pay in his hand. "What are you so mad about?" Jack asked him, still amazed at the man's attitude.

The captain sat down, and broke out crying. That was more amazing than anything that had happened yet! "I've known your parents for years," he wailed. "What will I tell them if you go off and get killed?"

Jack reached inside his breast pocket, pulled out a telegram, and put it on the table in front of the captain. It was a message from Jack's mother: God bless you boy, and good luck. If I was a man I'd go too.

After he'd read it, the captain got up, and shook Jack's hand. And the new private sent off to spend his pay.

Chapter 5
Rollin' Polly

The streets of Halifax were jammed as the soldiers marched down to the docks. The people along their route shouted and screamed and waved handkerchiefs as they passed.

"Bring us back a Boer's beard," a man shouted, and the people all around him cheered. Things weren't going well in South Africa. The first batch of troops that had gone out from Canada had thought that the war was just a picnic. Nobody realized the war would still be going on when they got there. But the Boers had fought well, and still surrounded British troops at three places: Ladysmith, Mafeking, and Kimberley. The second batch of troops were going from Halifax to South Africa to help out Britain — the mother country, Jack's parents said. That's why his mother was so delighted and proud when he signed up: "Britain needs you, Jack," he could imagine her saying.

They were getting near the docks now, and there, tied up at the government wharf, was the *Laurentian*. She was a ratty old steamship, and Jack looked around at the soldiers marching beside him. How many of them had ever been to sea? He smiled. Among sailors, the boat they were sailing on was not called the *Laurentian*, even though that was the name painted on bow and stern. Men that Jack knew called her the 'Rollin' Polly'. As he looked at the ship, Jack could smell a gale in the wind coming from the sea.

The 'Polly' cast off lines, and the men shouted good-byes to the people along the shore. The ship had begun to roll as they headed out, and soon after they left the wharf, the captain stopped engines, and the anchors rattled down. It was cool and wet, and the light was fading at the end of a cold, overcast day.

Below in the hold were the horses for the artillery. Everything had been loaded in haste so they could get away. Two more troopships were leaving in the next couple of days. So it was just as well, thought Jack, that the captain was giving the crew some time to organize things. For one thing, they had to make sure the horses would be all right. They were stalled in slings, that were suspended from great hooks and if they ever broke loose, the poor animals would be broken to pieces down there.

The next morning, Jack woke to the rattle of anchor chains, and for a while he lay still. After all, he'd left harbour many times before, and he was from Newfoundland, the home of many sailors. Newfoundland, itself, was a separate country. In 1867, they'd decided not to join Canada, and Newfoundlanders had gone their own way since.

He came out on deck just as the ship was moving out of the harbour. Halifax glided past, roofs bright in the morning, and the citadel on the crest of the hill looking like a long, low barracks. The water was choppy, and sun winked on the waves. He leaned on the rail, wondering how many more times he'd watch a harbour recede like this on his way out to sea. He'd see a lot of the world before he was through.

They were approaching the forts at the entrance to the harbour, and already the Atlantic was beginning to roll the *Laurentian*.

"It's a good morning," said one of the soldiers who'd come up from below.

"Looks it," said Jack. "Might be a blow later."

"I thought we waited it out."

"This is January," said Jack.

"I guess the ocean can get awfully bad?" asked the soldier.

"Can," Jack replied. The 'Polly' was already rolling pretty fair, with a kind of pitch and stagger that only a good sailor would be able to take for long. The first bit of spray flung itself over the bow, misted, and washed back along the side of the 'Polly'. Out to sea, the surface was heaving. The soldier had already gone back below, and Jack watched the sea a bit longer, then went down for breakfast. Some of the men were having a tough time just staying on the benches.

By that night, almost everyone was sick.

"I guess you're used to a lot worse," said the soldier he'd met on the deck in the morning.

"This is pretty bad," Jack replied. The way the fellow looked, it was no time to tell him what a really bad blow was like. The soldier lay in his hammock, and watched the deck above him sway back and forth, back and forth. Over three hundred men had hammocks pitched down there right above the dining tables. The long cave of the dining hall had become a sick bay, with the men slung above the tables, swinging back and forth.

An officer came to the bulkhead door and stuck his head in. He was wiry and leather faced, with a white moustache and goatee. "The horses have come loose and there's a lot of them lying in the hold," he announced. "I need some men to get them back in their slings. If we don't, they'll break their legs."

Jack stood up, but nobody else made a move. The officer made his way along the hammocks, glancing in each as he passed. When he came up to Randell, he said: "Looks like you're the only healthy man. You'd better come with me."

As he followed the officer, Jack figured that sometimes there were advantages to being seasick. On the other hand, if their horses were destroyed, they'd be a mounted infantry without mounts. He didn't relish walking when they got to South Africa, not when he could ride.

Water was sloshing in the hold. In the confusion of loading, refuse had got stuffed in the drainholes, and there was no place for the water to drain off. So every time a wave came aboard, it stayed — at least part of it. A number of the slings were draped loosely from the hooks. Some of the horses were lying in water amid the loose boxes and bales. Each pitch and toss of the seas forced them to scramble about.

"Careful they don't kick you," the officer warned. "I'll get some other men down here. See what you can do."

Jack bridled one of the closer animals, and bracing his feet, dragged it to a sling, steadied himself, and looped the bands underneath the animal.

This was a pretty poor job of stowing, he thought as he fixed the sling back in place. Shortly after, the officer returned with two more men.

"This is all, I'm afraid," he shouted, for the noise down here had become deafening. "Keep those animals as quiet as you can. I'll be back shortly."

"Who's that?" Randell asked one of the others.

" 'Gat' Howard," the fellow said. "He's a Yankee, out here with the Colt Arms Company. Trying to sell the British army a new colt machine gun."

They worked for forty-eight hours straight, 'Gat' Howard right beside them. Finally, when the seas let up, they stumbled off to sleep. They'd have to destroy a few of the horses, if the animals didn't get a lot better soon. Even so, most of them would survive.

As they climbed up the ladder to the upper deck, scruffy and unshaven, 'Gat' Howard turned and said: "I want to thank you men. We'd have lost them without you."

They were too tired to reply, and Jack slept right through the next day.

After that, the seas got calmer, and the weather much warmer. As they steamed south, the sun came out, and the men cheered as its first rays pierced through clouds and spotlighted the ocean far ahead of them.

On the last day of January, 1900, the *Laurentian* steamed into the harbour of San Vincent, Cape Verde Islands. A fleet of ships was scattered around the harbour, most of them loaded with troops for South Africa.

The Boers were still fighting.

A sleek British cruiser, the *Cambria*, dipped its flag at the *Laurentian*, and a long boat was winched down its side. Pulling on long sweeping oars, a company of British sailors, wearing blue jackets and white hats, rowed the boat across to the *Laurentian*. 'Rollin' Polly', thought Jack Randell, was too undignified a name for the *Laurentian* right now.

"Ahoy Canada," shouted a British officer at the stern of the longboat as they pulled alongside.

"What's the news?" several men shouted down.

"Your men are with Roberts chasing Boers," the officer shouted up.

"Have they caught any?" someone shouted.

"In good time," the officer replied.

"Is Ladysmith relieved?" shouted another.

"Not yet," the officer replied. "You'll have lots of fighting to do. We're saving a bit for you."

"Three cheers for the British Navy," hollered a voice, and the men shouted at the sailors, and the sailors cheered back.

After that, the sailing was smooth. The officers read, smoked pipes, or just watched the sea. Jack played poker.

They arrived in South Africa just as the first batch of Canadian soldiers, who had left two months earlier, were fighting the main Boer army far to the north.

Jack Randell felt good about that. Even though Newfoundland wasn't Canada, still, this lot of mainlanders wasn't all that bad.

Looming above the harbour and the town of Capetown was Table Mountain. It stretched like a huge coffin, steep up the sides, and flat like a table on top, with a fringe of cloud just above the crest. Beyond and above it all was the clean blue African sky.

Chapter 6
Horses

The last five weeks were the worst Jack Randell had ever spent in his life. His troop had been sent from Capetown along the railroad towards the interior. Then they had set off west, leaving the railroad. They crossed a desert, chasing some report about Boers in arms near Kenhart. Five weeks they had travelled through muddy creek beds where the wheels of the gun carriages sank deep in the muck, then out across long level stretches of desert under a baking sun, and then through sudden floods of rain. And always, just ahead of them, said the people they asked in the towns and lonely farms, were the Boers. They never saw any.

The final ten days had been the worst of all. They were ordered to push on as fast as they could to De Aar, and they marched with half rations. Jack's shoes, like many of the others, finally gave out, and he had to wrap oat sacks on his feet. He got so hungry he stole handfuls of grain from the horses, and crunched the horrible dry stuff, just to get something in his stomach. But it had been worse for the horses.

The horses would stagger as they pulled on a gun through some cursed dry creek bed, called a 'drift' here. Down a beast would go, tangled in the harness. The men would cut it loose, drag it to the side of the trail, and shoot the animal. There was no point letting it suffer.

Once in a while, some rider on the flanks would feel his animal giving out under him, He'd dismount, look at the beast, lead it forward a bit, and shake his head. Then he'd draw his pistol, stand back, and fire. The vultures had another meal.

They made good time, and got to De Aar twenty-four hours before they were supposed to.

But did they go anywhere? No. After all that marching, after starving themselves and shooting perfectly good horses that the army had driven into the ground, they sat here. How stupid, thought Jack, remembering how hard he had worked to save those very horses they had shot.

He was keeping a personal collection of lice. They were swarming in the sand where the officers had camped them. He'd never seen such insects so large.

"Is this what we came to Africa for?" asked one of his friends, squashing one of the insects.

"I want the two biggest you've got," said Jack.

"You can have them all," said the man, searching his clothes. "What I wouldn't do for a swim."

De Aar was the dustiest, driest place Jack Randell had ever seen. And here they were, stuck on guard duty, making sure nobody stole the railroad tracks, while every day trains passed by full of troops going north where the fighting was.

"Hand me that match box, will you?" Randell asked his friend, who passed it over. Then Jack got up, put something in the box, and strode to the major's tent.

During the march, the major had lost two good horses that he used to pull a cart with his equipment. Randell saluted, and handed the officer the box. "These ought to pull your cart better than any team I ever saw, Major."

The officer took the box, looked at Randell suspiciously, and opened it. Inside were two of the largest lice he had ever seen.

He flung his head back and roared with laughter.

Chapter 7
Laager

After a long stay at De Aar, they were ordered to march again. The railroad was for other people, the soldiers marched. Maybe it was because trains were short, thought Jack Randell, but it seemed a cruel joke that they had to slog along right beside the railroad tracks. At least he was lucky. He was part of the artillery, so he had to ride a horse to keep up with the gun carriages.

They were covered in dust. The soldiers sang to break the monotony, until they got tired and just marched. The columns of men spread out, the soldiers slung guns over their shoulders in whatever position seemed easiest, and the march straggled on.

Jack rode slack reined, glancing at the ground ahead to make sure the horse didn't stumble. It picked its own way pretty well.

"Where do you think we're going?" the fellow riding beside him asked.

"Haven't heard," Jack admitted. "Generals don't tell much to the likes of you and me."

"Probably it's just another march."

"To keep our spirits up," said Jack.

At a small station along the rail line, they stopped, and the major called the men together.

"We're marching to a place called Douglas, to the west of here. There's a bunch of Boers that have been causing trouble over there, and it's our job to flush 'em out."

They left the rail line, marched, stopped, marched, stopped once more, and then, at dusk, started on a night march.

At five in the morning, as the sky was beginning to glow with the coming sun, they camped. They were close to Douglas now, the centre of the Boer operations in the area. Jack rubbed his hands, and warmed them over one of the fires, then gulped down some hot tea. One of the great pleasures of life, he thought, is hot food when you're cold and working hard, He was feeling full of ginger this morning, and he blew in his hands to warm them.

In a minute, the sergeant came up.

"We're off."

Jack mounted, the others took their places on the gun carriages, and the column moved out again, heading west. The sun had risen behind them and lit the tops of the hills in front, which glowed in the yellow light. The air was getting slightly warmer.

A few miles from Douglas, Sam Hughes from Lindsay, Ontario, galloped in with a scouting party that had been sent on ahead. Almost at once, the major rushed over to the guns.

"There's a Boer wagon train drawn up in a circle just over those hills. Let's get 'em."

Jack whooped, and the men on the gun carriages lashed at their horses. Over stones, ruts and giant ant hills they crashed and bounded, and the men riding the gun carriages gripped the frames to keep themselves from being thrown off. Wind rushed in Jack's face. This was more like it! This was what he had come to South Africa for.

They rounded the hills, and off in the distance they saw the wagons. The men turned the carriages around, leaped off, and unhitched the guns. While some trained the guns on the Boer wagons, others pulled shells from shell boxes and rammed them into the gun breeches.

One gun fired, then another, then more, and the men rammed more shells home. The officers looked through their binoculars at the Boer wagons.

White smoke burst over the wagons, and fragments of shell spattered among them. More shells burst, and already the Boers were scurrying around, pulling wagons out of position and rushing oxen into their yokes.

The circle of the wagons broke to pieces in a storm of shell bursts. In ten minutes it was all over.

After days and days of marching, there had been no more than ten minutes of long distance shelling before the fighting was over. At least, though, Jack Randell had seen the Boers.

The column marched again, and entered the town of Douglas, but almost at once, reports came that the Boers were returning to the scene of battle to get the wagons they'd had to leave behind.

This time the soldiers rushed to the bank of a river just across from the Boer wagons. There was more firing and more shell bursts, now almost at point blank range. Then two or three dark figures started walking out of the Boer position towards the guns.

"Cease fire," shouted the major.

"Some women," said one of the men. Jack could make out the white sheet or flag or whatever it was they were waving. They had reached the bank of the river and they were sweeping their flags back and forth. Some soldiers splashed across the river on horses. The men bent down to listen to the women, and rode on towards the wagons. They returned, signalled for the men to advance, and the rest of the column was ordered across.

The wagons were punctured with shell fragments, and a couple of unshaven men were lying beside a wagon groaning with pain. Most of the Boers, though, had gotten away.

Chapter 8
Faber's Farm

A week after the fight at Douglas, they marched about 20 kilometres west, and camped overnight at a place called Faber's Farm. The Boers hung around the flanks of the column but kept their distance from the guns.

Jack woke the next morning so early that the ground was still dark with night, and the peaked white canvas tents were dim triangles laid out in rows. Soon, the bugle would blare reveille. Beyond the tents was the farmhouse that belonged to the man called Faber. Its wide roof and broad verandah looked homelike and peaceful in the midst of war. A number of twelve-pound shrapnel guns and machine guns aimed their muzzles at the sky in a ragged row.

The growing light picked out pebbles and stones on the ground outside the tents, and made long shadows of them. Jack Randell stirred in his blanket that was spread out on a ground sheet inside the tent. He was just barely awake.

Suddenly, he sat up. From all sides rifle shots snapped. Bullet holes punctured the tent all around the peak, and Jack threw himself prone. Bullets clattered against the gun barrels outside.

"Ambush!" Maybe he shouted it himself, maybe somebody else did, Jack couldn't tell. Horses screamed. Amid a chorus of wild yells, the panicky animals stampeded through the camp.

"Get the horses!" voices yelled.

Jack crawled out of the tent, scrambling on his elbows as rifle fire swept over the camp. He made it to the guns, and was quickly joined by the whole troop of artillery. They slammed shells in the chambers, set up the machine guns, and waited for orders. Over to one side, men were dragging the artillery horses to safety behind the farmhouse. Thank God the horses were still here, thought Jack.

"Looks like the Boers caught us good!" he remarked as they all waited for orders to open fire. There was a spatter of rifle fire to the right. The English troops were firing into an orchard nearby, where the Boers had hidden themselves.

"They got right into camp!" said one of the men at the guns. It was lucky they didn't wait till reveille, Jack realized. If they'd opened up when everybody was walking around, the whole troop would have been done for.

"Good men," said Sam Hughes, rushing up. "Hold your fire till we know where they are, so we can do the most good."

Bullets pinged around them, and a couple of men were hit. Still, the Canadians sat coolly by the guns, watching the fight like spectators.

"Are the horses all right?" asked Hughes.

"Over there," said Jack, pointing behind the farmhouse. The officer nodded in satisfaction. More men went down, but the rest of them sat, waiting for the order to fire. Soldiers were still rushing around among the tents, some of them not quite knowing where to go or what to do. Officers blew whistles to call them into line.

The Canadian gunners sat for an hour, more were wounded, and one man was killed. Then Hughes said: "All right. Get ready now."

The men got up, crouched behind their guns, and waited. Nobody could use the Colt machine guns, because the heavy fire had smashed their shields.

"Aim for the orchard," said Hughes, and the men adjusted their sights.

"Steady," said Hughes, his voice calm and professional.

"Fire."

Shells flew out of the barrels, the guns bucked, the men yanked the breeches open, rammed shells in, slammed the breeches closed, and fired again. Shrapnel rattled among the trees, and white bursts of smoke drifted off above the treetops. The rifle fire slackened almost at once.

"They're running."

"Limber!" hollered Sam Hughes. When they heard this order, men raced to the farmhouse, galloped the horses over, backed them into the traces, hitched them, and whipped off after the Boers.

Out beyond the orchard the gun carriages rattled, the men yelling, the horses' manes streaming. On a bit of rising ground, the men whirled the guns into position, aimed, and fired at the fleeing Boers. Some of the Boers dropped when the shrapnel burst, and the rest raced on out of sight.

When the officers counted their losses, they discovered that the column had lost twenty killed and a hundred wounded.

"The artillery saved the day," boasted Sam Hughes.

Jack and the others made no comment. Nobody had to tell them what they'd done. They knew.

Those Boers, Jack decided, were good fighters. It was pure luck that they hadn't wiped the column out. Among the dead were the sentries who had been guarding the camp, and according to one rumour, six of the best Boer marksmen had been picked to kill the commander, while others were selected to wipe out all the other officers.

We've still got things to learn about fighting, Jack thought.

Chapter 9
Howard's Canadian Scouts

After the fight at Faber's Farm, it was nothing but march, starve, almost die of thirst, eat corn out of the same nose bags as the horses, and set up camp among more lice. Every other troop of soldiers marched north where the fighting was. And then, when the Boer capital of Pretoria fell, everybody said the war was over.

But Jack remembered those Boers at Faber's Farm. They didn't give up easily, and they were still fighting.

Finally, the men in Jack's troop had gone to their officers and demanded: "Give us a fight or send us home." They announced that they were sending the men home.

That was why Jack was now sitting in a bar in Adderley Street, Capetown. "Where are your boys camped?" asked a soldier beside him.

"Just out of town," Jack replied. "We came in this morning, and they're putting us on the ship tomorrow. I've been off at the docks packing things up."

An officer strode into the bar, and asked to see the owner. When the owner appeared, the officer took him into a corner and whispered something, then strode out looking serious. In the distance there was the noise of singing men, and a few minutes later hundreds of soldiers poured into the bar. The clamour was unbelieveable. The owner climbed up on the bar, held his hands out, and, above the din, shouted: "I can't serve drinks to you, boys."

A roar of anger answered him.

"I can't help it," he pleaded. "An officer just came in. I have orders not to serve drinks."

"We'll take them!" the men hollered back, and the owner dove off the bar as shots shattered the mirrors and men clambered over the bar and started serving out drinks.

Then the crowd pushed outside and poured down the street towards the bar at the Grand Hotel. Officers raced ahead, and when the men shoved in, the owner was standing on his bar.

"Listen boys," he shouted, "they won't let me sell you a drink. But they can't stop me giving them away. The drinks are free as long as they last. The only thing I ask is, don't wreck the bar!"

The men cheered, and crowded up for drinks.

After a while, somebody said that 'Gatling Gun' Howard was in the hotel. He was raising an outfit of Canadian Scouts to carry on the fight with the Boers. So a group of men went up to his room, asked him to come down, and he was carried into the bar on their shoulders and hoisted up above the crowd.

He told them about the troop he was raising, and everybody shouted: "I'm going!"

He held up his hands. "See me later," he said. "I'll pick the best of the lot of you!" The men hollered themselves hoarse as he clambered down and pushed his way out.

By ten, the bar was dry, and the men passed around their hats for the owner. They gave him six hats full of gold sovereigns, and not more than six glasses had been broken all night.

As the men dispersed, Jack Randell went in search of 'Gat' Howard. In a small room in the attic of the Grand Hotel he found him. He knocked, walked in, stood to attention and saluted. "Major Howard, sir, I've come to join your scouts."

"Sit down," said Howard. "And don't call me major. Call me Gat."

Now here is a man to serve under, thought Jack, as he took a seat.

"Haven't I seen you somewhere before?" Howard asked after Randell was comfortable.

"Yes sir. We both came out on the old 'Rollin' Polly'."

"Of course," Howard said, smiling. "You're the fellow who saved my horse!" Randell remembered the

animal. It was a magnificent mount, and was evidently 'Gat' Howard's favourite. That forty-eight hours work on the old 'Polly' could turn out to be the best work he'd done during the war.

The major questioned him about his tour of duty in South Africa, and when Jack Randell rose at the end of the talk, Howard gripped his hand. "You'll be one of my scouts, Randell. You've got my word."

Fifty-five Canadians, and one Newfoundlander, were chosen, and every one had to prove he could ride without a saddle, shoot at the gallop, and hit what he shot at. They swaggered into Capetown, and bought whip-cord riding breeches, tight-fitted khaki tunics, high laced leather boots, and silver spurs. Howard gave each of them two long, single action .45 Colt revolvers, a carbine, and three horses: one to ride, and two to lead and shift to when the first was played out.

Two days after Christmas, 1900, Jack Randell boarded a train for Pretoria. He was now in Howard's Canadian Scouts, and proud of it, even though he wasn't Canadian. Newfoundland, after all, was a separate country.

Now he'd get some real fighting. All fifty-six of them would.

He was right. Three months later, only four of them would be left alive.

Chapter 10
Fight at the Corral

Soon after they arrived at Pretoria, they joined General French, who was leading eleven huge columns of soldiers to the east. His aim was to sweep the whole country and collect every Boer fighter he could find. The British army now controlled all the cities and towns, but the Boers were fighting on in small bodies called commandos. They raided the army whenever they could, and then went back to their farms where they got food and other supplies to carry on the fight.

That's all they can do, thought Jack. There's thousands of us, and only hundreds of them. The army's orders were to collect all the women and children in the farms, and bring them into camps where they'd be watched. The farms were to be burned.

Jack was now riding with a group of the Scouts half way between Pretoria and Piet Retief. Twenty kilometres behind was the main column of soldiers. The Scouts were out in front, searching for the Boers.

They'd been moving now for several hours, under a high, blazing sun. Over the whole country, not a human being moved. Then ahead on a gentle rise, four riders rode into sight, stopped, and watched them.

"Yoicks and away!" shouted one of the Scouts. It was a cry used in England by fox-hunters. Captain Ross, riding his horse in front, swept his hand in the direction of the Boers, chopped his spurs into his horse, and they followed him yelling and whooping.

The riders on the crest of the hill sat on their horses calmly, and as the men got close, they raised their rifles and fired. They remained there as the Scouts got closer, and then they wheeled, and disappeared over the crest.

Twenty-five Scouts, spread out in line abreast, charged over the slight hill. There, waiting for them, was a commando of about a hundred and fifty Boers.

They'll wipe us out, thought Jack Randell. But Ross shouted: "Smash through them and turn back!" He kept riding straight at the Boers.

It's the only thing to do, thought Randell. If we turn now, they'll smash us. The only chance we have is to charge straight through. He dropped the reins of his horse, yanked out his revolvers, and blazed away at full gallop. Men dropped on both sides of him, some Boers went down, and then the Scouts drove into the Boer line. Men tumbled from their horses, powder burns on their shirts from guns fired at point blank range.

The Scouts were behind the Boers now. The Boer commandos swung their horses about as Ross wheeled, hollered 'Charge', and spurred back at the Boers.

Gripping his horse's flanks with his knees, Jack Randell followed, his Colts banging as more men tumbled out of their saddles.

They were through the Boer line again which was now jumbled and disorganized. Five of us left, thought Jack Randell, looking around.

"Make for that farm," shouted Ross. About two kilometres ahead was a stone farmhouse, and beside it was a horse corral surrounded by a stone wall. They pounded for the corral, and the Boers followed, coming on with guns blazing.

The five remaining Scouts halted, swung around, and shot at the Boers with their carbines. Their pursuers pulled up. Then the Scouts whirled, and dashed for the corral again. After going some distance, they stopped once more and turned.

Jack levelled his carbine, and suddenly the earth seemed to leap at him and whack him in the face. He got up, saw that his horse had been shot out from under him, and looked around. He still had his carbine.

"Grab my stirrup," hollered Ross. Jack raced over, seized the stirrup of Ross's mount just as the captain spurred his horse. Running beside him, gripping the stirrup desperately, Jack felt himself leaping enormous steps.

At the stone wall, the horse bounded and Jack sailed over beside it, not quite knowing how he'd done it. He let go of the stirrup, and almost ran through the wall on the other side. Then he raced back to the wall nearest the Boers, and continued shooting at them. They stopped, dismounted, and started crawling forward, firing as they came. One by one, Jack and the remaining Scouts picked them off.

Still the Boer fire poured in. How long can the five of us hold them off, Jack wondered.

"Hey!" somebody shouted. Far across the level plain, a column of dust billowed into the clear sky. It was the rest of the army. Jack and the others cheered, yelled, pounded each other, and blazed away at the Boers once more.

The Boers had seen the cloud also. Crawling back to their horses, they mounted and rode off.

Thirsty! — Jack's throat was parched.

On one of the horses that had followed them in was a canteen. Jack yanked it off, hoisted it to his lips, and gulped great huge mouthfuls of water. When it was empty, he closed his eyes, and heaved a great sigh.

Once he'd rested a bit, he took one of the extra horses, mounted up, and rode over with the others to see if anyone out there was still alive.

He came up to a figure in khaki stretched out on the ground. The man had been shot through the body, and it looked like he was dead. Jack dismounted. It was Sergeant Munsey, one of his chums. The front of his shirt was bloody, just above his heart, and Jack felt the man's chest. It was moving — Old Munsey was alive!

Jack bounded up, grabbed a canteen, poured some rum into it, and held it up to Munsey's lips. The sergeant spat, gulped, and came to. He looked around. "Where's my clothes?" he asked. The Boers had stripped him to his shirt. His spurs, boots, tunic, trousers, Colts and carbine were gone. He lay back cursing. Old Munsey was alive all right!

When the rest of the soldiers came in, they put Munsey on a stretcher and took him away. As Jack Randell rode off, he turned and looked back at the farmhouse. Black smoke was roiling up. Someone had set it afire.

Chapter 11
The Ride in the Dark

The march through Boer territory continued, and the camps where the army took the women and children grew all along the route of the march. Crops were razed, food storage destroyed, and farmhouses burned. And, hanging around the flanks of the columns, were countless Boer commandos.

Jack Randell was promoted to sergeant, and led small scouting parties in front of one of the columns. The Boers sniped at them when they got the chance, then vanished as the main column came up. Randell's days were filled with small alarms.

He'd just returned from a scouting trip when 'Gat' Howard called him to his tent. As Randell dismounted, the major came out carrying a long, official looking envelope. "These are despatches for General French. I want you to get them over to him, Jack. Hand them to him personally. He's across the Assagai River, near Piet Retief."

"Right now?" asked Randell.

"After dark," Howard ordered. "There's bound to be a Boer commando or two between here and there. It's too dangerous during daylight. Take another Scout with you."

The sky had been overcast that day, and the night came on dark and early. As Jack rode out of camp, he flipped open his pocket compass to check his bearings. If I can reach one of the fords on the Assagai, he thought, I should get across pretty quick. Snapping his compass shut, he stuffed it in his pocket and changed direction a bit. The other Scout followed, and they spurred their horses into an easy gallop. Rain began spotting the ground, and suddenly the sky dumped a flood on their heads. Great drops drummed on the ground, and the black was so dense you could almost feel it. They slacked up their pace a bit, but still moved on at a good canter. The thrumming of the rain blotted out the sound of their horses' hooves.

Jack's clothes felt as if they were pasted to his skin. But with all he'd been through, a little rain didn't hurt much. He could get used to almost anything.

They'd ridden for a couple of hours, and it was still raining heavily when someone in front hollered: "Halt!" It was English, but the sound of it meant only one thing — a Boer.

Jack turned in his saddle, said, "Keep up with me" to the man behind him, and jammed his spurs in the horse. It bounded ahead.

A rifle flashed and cracked. The Boer missed and jumped out of the way as Jack came right down on top of him. The flash of gunfire winked all around. We've come straight into their camp, Jack thought, as hoarse Dutch shouts clamoured in the dark. Suddenly his horse gave a great lunge, and the ground became air underneath him. They fell, almost floated, and a great splash rushed in his ears.

Water covered him. Then he started to rise, and he could feel his horse struggling back to the surface of the water. They broke surface and he gulped air as bullets kicked the water around him.

He was right in the middle of the Assagai River. Ahead he could make out the dark hilly shore on the other side. He slid off the saddle, stretched himself prone, and held on the saddle horn. The horse could swim better, he figured, if it didn't have the weight of a man to carry. He turned its head to the far bank.

Behind him he could hear the other Scout floundering in the water, and the angry shouts of the Boers, and the spatter of bullets on the river. His horse's feet found land, he pulled himself back in the saddle, and the animal dragged itself up the bank, blowing from the effort of the swim. Bullets still hummed by. Jack spurred on, heard the other scout following, and they both vanished in the dark. After a while, he reined in. The other Scout caught up, and they waited for a moment. There was no sound of pursuit. Jack flicked his mount, and they started on.

About two o'clock, an English voice shouted: "Halt!"

Jack pulled up. There was no sense coming all this way just to get shot by one of your own men.

"Two of Howard's Canadian Scouts," he shouted, "with despatches for General French."

"Come ahead," shouted the sentry, sounding suspicious, and Jack cantered his mount slowly forward. The sentry held his rifle steady, aiming it straight at Jack's heart. Then, satisfied with the look of these two bedraggled figures in khaki, the sentry lowered his gun and said: "All right." The corporal of the guard emerged out of the dark, looked the two men over, and led them to a tent. As he dismounted, Jack thought: well, we've made it.

A kerosene lamp was flaring on the table and the white oval of its light was framed by the inverted V of the tent entrance. A solemn looking soldier, his moustache carefully trimmed, and his back rigid, stood by the table.

"Give me your despatches," he said.

On the man's sleeve were the stripes of a sergeant-major. Looking directly at them, Jack Randell asked: "Are you General Sir John French?"

Erect with the importance of his uniform, the man replied in a thickish accent: "No." He paused, ran his eyes up and down Jack's mud-caked, dripping, soggy uniform. "But I am the Brigade Sergeant-Major. You will give me your despatches."

Oh will I? thought Jack. He was sure that half of that thick accent was put on, just for effect. But, whether it was or wasn't, Jack Randell was not going to hand over his despatches to any pompous British Sergeant-Major.

"My despatches are for the hands of General French alone. I am to give them to him alone."

"You will give them to me, sergeant," demanded the fellow. Jack refused, and they argued about it.

Hearing the shouts, General French came in from the next tent. He was short, almost square shaped, but his eyes swept the tent and took in the situation at once. Randell and the others snapped to attention. Reaching inside his tunic, Jack drew out the sopping envelope, and handed it, still dripping, to General French.

"You appear slightly damp, Sergeant," French said to Randell.

"Yes sir," Jack replied. "We rode through a Boer camp on the way over and landed in the Assagai River."

"Did you kill any of them?" French asked.

"I tried to run them down sir, but I didn't stop because I thought it was better to get these despatches through.

"Good work," said French, chuckling. He turned the envelope over, gauged its weight, and looked up at the Sergeant-Major. "Get these men some hot food and rum." Then he turned and walked out.

The Sergeant-Major grumbled as he gave orders to bring some food and rum. Randell and the other Scout looked at each other, and smirked.

They never found out what those despatches said. When they got back, 'Gat' Howard said something about military secrecy, and thanked them both. Jack Randell had learned, however, that war was like that. It was either a complete waste of time, or it was so secret that nobody told the ordinary soldier what was going on.

Chapter 12
A Ride in the Mountains

When General French had finished his march, countless farmhouses had been burned, and a number of camps had been set up for Boer women and children. The fighting, however, did not end. If anything, it got more fierce.

Howard's Canadian Scouts were sent out on a separate mission to track down a Boer commando unit that was reported to be collecting in a mountainous area. They found nothing.

Major Howard, along with his orderly, had gone ahead to scout out the terrain. Jack Randell rode with the rest of the men along the side of a rocky valley. Far across on the other side, they could see small figures among the rocks. They fired at them, and the sound echoed across the valley. The Boers disappeared, and the Scouts rode on.

There didn't seem to be any hurry, and Jack was enjoying the sun and the cooler air in the mountains. It was good to get away from the flat plain and the dust and heat. If they didn't get some Boers, there might be some other game. This war was like some kind of hunting party.

Hooves clattered furiously along the trail up ahead and Major Beatty, his eyes full of haste and panic, charged around the flank of the hill.

" 'Gat' Howard's in trouble," he shouted, whirled his horse, and raced off, with Jack and the others behind him.

As they rounded the flank of the next hill, they came on a steep valley, and there, near a rocky ridge half way up the other side, were Boer wagons.

"They've got him up there," shouted Beatty, pointing at the wagons, as bullets sang off the rocks around them.

Jack hopped off his mount, his carbine gripped in his right hand, and dashed for the nearest rock. The men scattered along the side of the valley and started working their way down, rushing from rock to rock Indian style. Jack popped up, snapped a shot at the Boers far above the wagons on the ridge, ducked as bullets whanged off a rock, crouched, and rushed for the next bit of cover. Beside the rock where he threw himself was a bit of stick. He reached out, dragged it over, and clapped his hat on it. Then, slowly, he raised it above the rock. He eased over to one side, holding his hat out in sight, well away from his head. A man appeared from behind cover on the other side and drilled a hole in the hat, just before Jack Randell shot him. The Boer fell over, his rifle spewing down the slope, and he lay inert. Jack rushed for the next rock.

They crossed the valley that way, and made their way up the other side towards the wagons. As they went up, Jack and three others worked over on the flank of the Boers until they'd caught them in a crossfire.

Suddenly, the firing stopped. Jack kept down, then slowly eased his head up. There was no sign of movement up there. Then, high up, a man suddenly appeared, running. Jack snapped a shot at him.

He was too far away. Then a few others appeared, and the group vanished over the ridge. Still, Jack couldn't be sure. He glanced over at the others,

squatting behind rocks. Then one of the men raised himself a bit, dashed ahead, and scrambled into cover.

Nothing.

A few more tried it, and still nothing happened. Slowly, Jack eased himself up, crouched, ran ahead and, when he hadn't been shot at, started moving ahead more openly keeping low.

But the Boers had gone. They reached the wagons with no more trouble.

These were typical Boer wagons, heavy and awkward, with a cylinder of canvas looped over the body of each. Fresh chips were knocked out of the grey unpainted sides by the bullets. Some boxes had been smashed open. There was nothing else around except a bird, high up, turning on the wind that lifted over the ridge —

Nothing but a man, around whom they all gathered. His body was riddled with bullets, and many of them had been fired at such close range that there were powder burns on his shirt.

It was 'Gat' Howard.

Chapter 13
Duel

For Jack Randell, the war would never be the same. He led more scouting parties, and they ambushed Boers, and were ambushed in turn. The war had become very personal, man against man. Jack figured he had now become as good at fighting as the Boers.

Once again, he was leading a scouting party on another march in advance of a column. They were well out in front, and he'd told his men to spread out so they could cover more ground. He was riding alone down a rocky gully. Bushes, scrub grass, and boulders were scattered around. This country seemed so empty!

Bullets whinged off some rocks beside the trail. Jack dove to the ground, grabbing his carbine as he did. The horse was dead, but Jack was already crawling on elbows and knees for the closest rock as fast as he could scramble. Shots rang around him, and he tried to judge where they were coming from, even as he made for cover.

Carefully, he placed his hat on top of the rock and peeked around the side in the direction he decided the shots had come from. A couple of Boers were peering from behind a boulder some distance away. He snapped two quick shots at them, pulled his head back in, and waited until they stopped firing back. His hat had been knocked off the rock. He dragged it over with his foot, and found three bullet holes in it. He took another quick shot, the Boers fired back, but nobody was hit. They know what they're doing, Jack thought.

For half an hour the game went on, with no results on either side. Then Jack's men charged on the scene, the Boers dashed for their horses that had been hidden behind some rocks farther back, and galloped off to the rattle of fire from Randell's men.

The Scouts came back from the chase, and by now Jack had taken stock of his situation. "Go on scouting," he told them, before they could dismount. "There's a farmhouse over there. I'll walk over and sleep there tonight. The column will catch up with me tomorrow."

They gave him a half salute, turned their horses, and continued their scouting. Jack slung his canteen and saddle bags over his shoulder, and started off for the farmhouse.

It was about twenty kilometres of pretty hot slogging across the open plain, and Jack had a lot of time for thinking. Gradually, he figured, they were wearing the Boers down. The British held all the cities, towns and railroad lines. They were bringing in all the families from the outlying farms, so there were now no homes for the commandos to go to for supplies. Along all the railroad lines, the army had begun to build a line of barbed wire and blockhouses. The British were cutting the country up into blocks. Then, when they had sealed off a large block of country, they sent great columns searching for all the Boers they could find. If a man figured out how many square kilometres there were in the whole country, and how long it took to search out each square kilometre, he could know, almost exactly, how much longer the war was going to last.

But for a soldier like Jack Randell, who had to go out and find the Boers, the war was personal. Your horse got shot, you scrambled for cover, and you slogged it back on foot. And, the way the war was going now, it was kill or be killed.

Six hours after he had started, as the sun was getting low in the sky, Jack arrived at the farmhouse. The roof was still on, but the windows and everything inside had been smashed up. Even so, it was someplace to stay. When the column came tomorrow, they'd see the house and head for it, simply because it was the only thing around to see.

He kicked some broken glass out of the way, and looked at some bullet holes in the plaster. Whether they were Boer or British, he couldn't tell. The Boers were using guns they captured from the British anyway. If they wanted bullets, they just followed a big British wagon train. Soldiers were always throwing bullets away — why, Jack didn't know. So all a Boer had to do was pick them up, load his rifle, and fire them back at the soldiers who had dropped them.

Back in a rear room he found a mattress and flung down his saddle bags and canteen. He took his bandoliers off his shoulder and laid them out on the floor. He had lots of ammunition left. Then he sat down, drained half of the canteen, and pulled some biscuits out of his saddle bags.

Hard biscuits and water — you got used to it after a while, but that didn't mean you had to like it, The biscuit was so dry it'd shrivel the insides of your stomach if you didn't have water to wash it down.

Well now, Jack thought, I just wait. He stretched out, using his saddle bags for a pillow, and stared at the ceiling for a while. Then he rolled on his side and slept.

He woke suddenly. It was pitch dark and rain was pouring loudly on the ground outside. Vivid lightning briefly lit the room and thunder cracked overhead.

In the next room, he heard two voices. Jack eased off the mattress and started for the door very carefully. They were talking Dutch, and he understood enough to gather they had been passing by and had come in to get out of the storm. It was only a matter of time before they found him. At this stage in the war, nobody was taking prisoners. It was a question now of who would fire first, because the man that did would be the man that would get out of this alive.

Jack eased his pistols out of their holsters. They were loaded, because he hadn't used them in the fight earlier today, and he always kept his guns loaded anyway.

He was at the door now. Carefully, he got up, and laid himself flat against the wall just behind the door jamb. With the next glare of lightning, he saw them, and fired.

He'd hit one of them for he'd seen him fall in that wild instant, but the other man was still alive. He was also a good shot, for he had just missed Jack.

A shot rang out and Jack fired at the flash. Silence.

Careful, Jack thought, I can't let my breathing give me away. Despite the excitement, I have to keep my breathing even and quiet. Just one sound will give me away, and this fellow won't miss.

Another shot broke the silence. Jack fell, and lay still. Maybe he thinks he's got me, Jack thought. I'll wait until he comes over to have a look, and then I'll fire. But the fellow did not move.

Then Jack thought he heard a noise, and fired. He moved away at once, just as a pistol flashed again. He shot at the flash.

A thud.

Did I get him?

Randell listened. No sound, no breathing. But he sensed that something was wrong. He's pretending he's dead, he's pulling the same trick on me that I tried to pull on him!

Jack held one of his pistols far out to the side. I'll fire, he thought, and when he replies, I'll shoot at the flash with the other gun. He did that — and missed. He's pulling the same stunt I am!

Careful, thought Randell. Your breath is getting too loud. You've got to control yourself completely. But his heart was pounding with the strain, and his lungs felt like exploding. He controlled himself with a great effort of will. Then he held one of his guns far out to the side.

Maybe, he thought, the last time he almost got me was just luck. Maybe he hasn't guessed what I'm trying to do after all.

He shot, there was a flash, he shot at the flash and shifted away, just as another bullet passed close by his ear.

He almost got me!

The duel went on, and on. Jack tried every trick he knew, and so did the other man. The whole war was now down to two men in one house, neither of whom could hit the other. It was a stalemate. But some time, Jack thought, somebody will get lucky, because only one of us will walk out of here alive.

Slowly, he worked his way back to the doorway where he'd fired the first shot. Without making the slightest sound, he stretched himself flat on the floor. Then he carefully brought his pistol up until it pointed just past the edge of the door jamb into the next room. He squinted along the sight, and strained with all the strength he could muster in order to see. In all this time, there had not been one flash of lightning, not since the flash that had opened the fight. Surely we're due for one, he decided.

No sound. Not a breath, not the scrape of a shoe, not a cough, not even the blink of an eyelash, which Jack was sure he could have heard if it had happened.

Lightning glared. The other man was leaning forward around the corner of the door on the other side of the room. One, two, three shots. The pistol bucked in Jack's hand, then it was dark again. There was a thud, but now a gun rattled on the floor. The way that fell, thought Jack, was no trick.

Still, he was taking no chances. Holding the pistol cocked and ready in one hand, he struck a match with the other.

It was no trick. The other man was dead.

As long as I live, thought Jack, breathing freely now, I'll never forget this night.

Chapter 14
Jack Leaves South Africa

Soon after that, Jack's tour of duty ended. As he sat in the railroad coach, waiting for the train to start him on his long trip home, he was glad he was going. Framed outside the window of the passenger car was Pretoria, and this would be the last Jack would see of it. The war was still on, but there was less and less fighting, and it was gradually fading out. Even so, men were still dying in private battles, in sudden attacks and bitter fights, out in the country.

But for Jack, it was over. Two years in South Africa was enough.

The train eased forward, stopped, and then the conductor shouted the signal. They were off, gathering speed, rolling away from Pretoria, back to the sea, down to the ships — and home.

"Come on Jack," ordered one of the men, "where's those cards?"

"So you think you can play cards, now?" Jack asked, drawing a deck from his tunic pocket, and arching his eyes at the men opposite. "What's the stakes?" They'd been paid, and there wasn't much to spend it on, so the stakes would be high. Maybe, thought Jack, I'll have a real bankroll when I roll into Trinity, Newfoundland.

The game got started and went on, win and lose, for hours, even as they approached the long bridge over the Orange River at Norval's Pont. As he put down a card and won the hand, Jack Randell thought: I'm going to try for captain when I get home. One of these days, I'll have my own ship.

THE TEACHER

Chapter 15
Norval's Pont

The train carrying Jack Randell pounded across the bridge at Norval's Pont, passing under a series of curved steel arches that helped to hold the steel frame of the bridge rigid. A stone blockhouse stood near the bridge, and a couple of soldiers peered out the firing slits of the blockhouse at the passing train. They watched as the train steamed off down the track and dwindled to a black dot in the distance. The whistle gave one last, lonely blast and the soldiers watched until the only sign of the train was distant white smoke against the vivid blue African sky.

There was nothing else to do but watch trains pass. These men had the job of guarding the railroad bridge at Norval's Pont, and they roasted under a tin roof in the South African sun.

Near the blockhouse was a military camp for units of the British army. Every once in a while a column of soldiers would march off across the African plain, searching for Boers. Often, the column would come back without having seen any Boers at all, even though every soldier knew for certain that the Boers were hiding in the distant hills, waiting for a chance to attack. Sometimes, the crates on the wagons that followed along with the column would come loose, and a few rifle bullets would be shaken out. Once the column had passed, Boer horsemen would ride out where it had gone by, and search for the fallen bullets. While one man kept watch in case a troop of British cavalry attacked, the rest dismounted and collected the bullets. Then they would remount, and distribute the bullets among the others. Since most Boers now used captured British rifles, the bullets fit their guns perfectly. Without knowing it, the British army helped to keep the Boers supplied with ammunition.

The war went on, and on, and on. A full year after Jack Randell's train had passed over the bridge at Norval's Pont, there were still Boer commandos out in the hills beyond the river.

Early on the morning of Friday, June 6, 1902, a train arrived from the south. It squealed to a stop, and four women got out. The train was made up mostly of freight cars carrying supplies to the towns and cities farther north. But, coupled in the middle of the train, were two passenger coaches. A long white sign hung from each of the coaches, and on these signs some railroad workers had painted: "Contents: Canadian Teachers."

Maud Graham, one of the teachers, shouted goodbye to her friends, who were staying on the coaches and going to camps and towns farther north. Maud had a broad face and brown, friendly eyes. Her carefully brushed hair was caught back behind her head in a bun, and her dress was clean and neatly pressed despite the dust of the African plain. She shouted, "You've promised to write, Annie, now don't you forget. I'll be angry with you if you do. Goodbye Winnifrid. . . . "

Steam hissed from the steam engine, and the train slid forward and picked up speed. Out of every window in the passenger coaches, young women teachers leaned out. Maud suddenly felt very lonely. She had become fast friends with all these young women on the long trip from Canada to South Africa, and she knew that she would never see most of them again. "Goodbye — goodbye" was shouted from dozens of teachers on the train, and they all began singing a popular song: 'Good Bye Dolly Gray'. The train reached the bridge and picked up speed until it curved out of sight and the only sign of its passing was the steam lunging towards the sky and the voices singing, "Goodbye, Dolly Gray. . . goodbye Dolly Gray. . . goodbye. . . . "

Maud stared at the long shining rails, and the barbed wire that surrounded the nearby military camps.

It was frosty, and Maud and the other three women were hungry. They hammered on the door of the station and it rattled like the bones of a skelton. Soon an unshaven officer stuck his head out an upstairs window. "We're the new teachers from Canada," Maud shouted up. "It's cold out here, and we'd like to get inside to warm up, if we may."

"Right," answered the man, and he drew his head back in. In a moment, they could hear him clattering down the stairs inside, and then the door opened. They bustled in, and Maud exclaimed, "My, but it gets cold in the mornings."

"Might I see your permits?" he asked, and they gave him their military passes.

To control the movement of people within the areas they held, the British army issued passes, which people had to produce on demand, to make sure that they were not spies. In addition, they had brought all the Boer women and children from the farms into refugee camps. But, when these people had been brought there, they were crowded together in unsanitary conditions, and thousands of them died of disease.

That was why Maud and the others were here. When the deaths began to occur, the British sent in nurses to tend for the sick and dying, and when the epidemics were over, they asked for volunteers to help teach the children at the schools set up by the army. Maud had joined a group of one hundred teachers sent from Canada.

Once they had warmed themselves, Maud and the others set out by cart for the refugee camp at Norval's Pont. There was a high hill separating the military camp from the refugee camp, and as the cart rounded the slope, Maud was astonished. It was strange that a refugee camp should be in such a beautiful setting.

On the left were large hills, and the Orange River flowed along their base. On the right, the camp sloped up the opposite hillside. Long lines of white tents gleamed in the morning sun. Lines of white-washed stones lined the broad streets between the tents.

But then Maud thought of the women and children who had died here of disease, before the camp had been cleaned up and a sufficient supply of medical supplies brought in. She would have to help repair the damage, and the best way, was to give to the children of these people what she could of her best: her teaching abilities.

Chapter 16
A Ragged Ostrich Feather

On Monday morning, Maud Graham walked from her tent to the school. Thirteen hundred children: it was hard to believe there were that many little Boers in this camp. But when she walked into the school room, it was easy enough to believe. Although there were many other teachers here, she had 130 children to look after.

The children were just finishing a morning hymn. The Boers were a very religious people, and they had needed their religion to give them strength during the last two years. The children's voices were high, but already they had mastered the kind of serious chanting sound used by their parents as they finished 'Dare to be a Daniel'. Daniel in the lion's den — maybe, Maud thought, the women and children in this camp felt like they were in a British lion's den. Their homes and their crops had been burned, and many were very poor.

The little girls wore long dresses, and bonnets, and curiously, short-fingered mittens. For some strange reason, even though they lived in such a sunny country, they didn't like to have their hands and faces sun-burnt. And the boys, thought Maud: they all looked like small men. They had soft shapeless hats with the brims turned down, and their trousers were mostly of a mud-coloured corduroy. Their coats came up high on their necks, and had no collars. Their pants were short, reaching just above their boot tops. And the shoes — both the boys and the girls — were home-made, rather shapeless, but tough and comfortable. They called them 'veldt-shoene': shoes for the plain.

When the hymn was finished, a Dutch-speaking assistant started to read out the roll:

"Wilhelmina Kachelhoffer."

"Present." The child's voice, thought Maud, seemed awkward with the English word.

"Abraham Oosthuisen."

"Present."

While the list was read out, Maud went around examining feet, hands, necks, and ears. In a camp like this, where everybody had lived in tents for over a year, sickness spread very rapidly. In fact, hundreds of women and children had died here from disease. More women and children had died this way than men had died fighting the British.

To help keep up the health of the camp, the British army gave out soup at recess to all the children. A hospital had been set up within the camp, and a huge vegetable garden supplied abundant food.

Children, thought Maud, are so often the real victims of war. But at least they were getting some schooling — as much, anyway, as she could offer by herself, with one assistant, to 130.

The list was finished, and Maud went to the front of the class.

"Could you get out the slates," she asked her assistant. Six children walked to the cupboard, and took the slates from the Dutch girl, and handed them out. As one of the little girls passed Maud, she smiled shyly, and Maud beamed at her and brushed the little girl's hair with her hand.

They gave such sad little presents, these children. Maud had received a ragged ostrich feather from the little girl who had passed by smiling just now. Another gave a battered Christmas card, and another, the brightly coloured cover of a cigarette box. But she took them all with delighted thank-yous, and felt as happy as if a royal Duchess had given her a gold ring. At the end of each day, some of them stayed around and quarreled over who was to carry the teacher's clock back to the teacher's tent. And always, there was a bright little row of young ones to take her hand.

By now, the children were bending over their slates, copying letters from a blackboard set up on a stand at the front of the room.

At least thought Maud, they had a room, not a tent, like most of the other classes. It was a room in a rattly tin building — my, how it rattled when a midday wind came up and flung the roof up and down, and made such a racket they had to close school for the day. The floors were mud, hard packed mud, a bit dusty maybe, but they made no noise at all. At least that was one advantage over the noisy hardwood floors in the schools of Canada!

Maud went around the room once more, this time bending over the shoulder of each child, checking the work.

"Good, very good," she crooned at a serious little boy who bent over his slate as if nothing else existed.

"You must be more careful," she warned a chubby little girl, who was more interested in being liked by the teacher than doing her work. But now the girl scrunched over the work, because the teacher didn't like it.

"No," Maud said firmly to a boy who didn't care at all. She made him rub his work out and start again.

When she had checked them all, it was time to stop, because the children were getting restless. You couldn't expect such little ones to work as long as the older classes.

"Now sit up," she said brightly, "and we will have our reading lesson."

It happened, as it always did, every day. As soon as the children had laid down their slates and sat up straight for the reading lesson, a number of their benches collapsed. The benches often folded up without warning.

Already a child was crying because his toe had gotten badly pinched when the bench made itself flat.

"Miss Graham," a girl cried, "Wilhelmina is hurt." The assistant went over to Wilhelmina while Maud unfolded the bench and freed the boy.

When the confusion had ended, they started the reading lesson, repeating together the words written on a great sheet of paper pinned up at the front of the class.

Judging from the sound of their voices, Maud soon decided that they had had enough. So they all stood up and sang.

The children loved this, and she was amazed how quickly these little Dutch-speaking children picked up English songs, especially the ones that had lots of action. Children, she thought, are the same all over.

A bell clanged to announce recess. Rummaging in their bags, the children got out a mug or basin, depending on what their mothers had sent, and lined up for the soup. Maud had found that it was really quite good, and often took a bowl herself. She watched the little faces pass by her at the door — happy faces, serious faces, the faces of children who had had no hatred and a whole life ahead of them. Children who were children, even in war.

Later that same month, a group of ragged Boer men rode into the camp at Norval's Pont. After two and a half long years, and a war that had lasted two years longer than anybody had expected, peace had been signed. The men dismounted, stacked their guns in a great pile before the commander of the British troops, and then rode on to find their women and children.

The war ended quietly. The people packed, and left the camp in single families, or in groups. Some of them paused by the graves of women or children who had died at the camp, said nothing, and passed on.

I am glad the war is over, thought Maud. She would be staying in South Africa for at least a year, and now she would really be able to help make a peace. But she was sad to see the children of Norval's Pont go, for she would never see them again.